Sleep Tight, Little One

SLEEP TIGHT, LITTLE ONE
A Collection of Stories for Bedtime

LITTLE TIGER PRESS
An imprint of Magi Publications
1 The Coda Centre, 189 Munster Road,
London SW6 6AW
www.littletigerpress.com

First published in Great Britain 2008
This volume copyright © Magi Publications 2008
Cover illustration copyright © Alison Edgson 2008

LITTLE BEAR'S SPECIAL WISH
Gillian Lobel
Illustrated by Gaby Hansen
First published in Great Britain 2003
by Little Tiger Press
An imprint of Magi Publications
Text copyright © Gillian Lobel 2003
Illustrations copyright © Gaby Hansen 2003

NEWTON
Rory Tyger
First published in Great Britain 2001
by Little Tiger Press
An imprint of Magi Publications
Text and Illustrations copyright
© Rory Tyger 2001

HAVE YOU GOT MY PURR?
Judy West
Illustrated by Tim Warnes
First published in Great Britain 1999
by Little Tiger Press
An imprint of Magi Publications
Text copyright © Judy West 1999
Illustrations copyright © Tim Warnes 1999

GOODNIGHT, LITTLE HARE
Sheridan Cain
Illustrated by Sally Percy
First published in Great Britain 1999
by Little Tiger Press
An imprint of Magi Publications
Text copyright © Sheridan Cain 1999
Illustrations copyright © Sally Percy 1999

Sleep Tight, Little One

A Collection of Stories for Bedtime

LITTLE TIGER PRESS

Contents

LITTLE BEAR'S
SPECIAL
WISH

GILLIAN LOBEL

illustrated by

GABY HANSEN

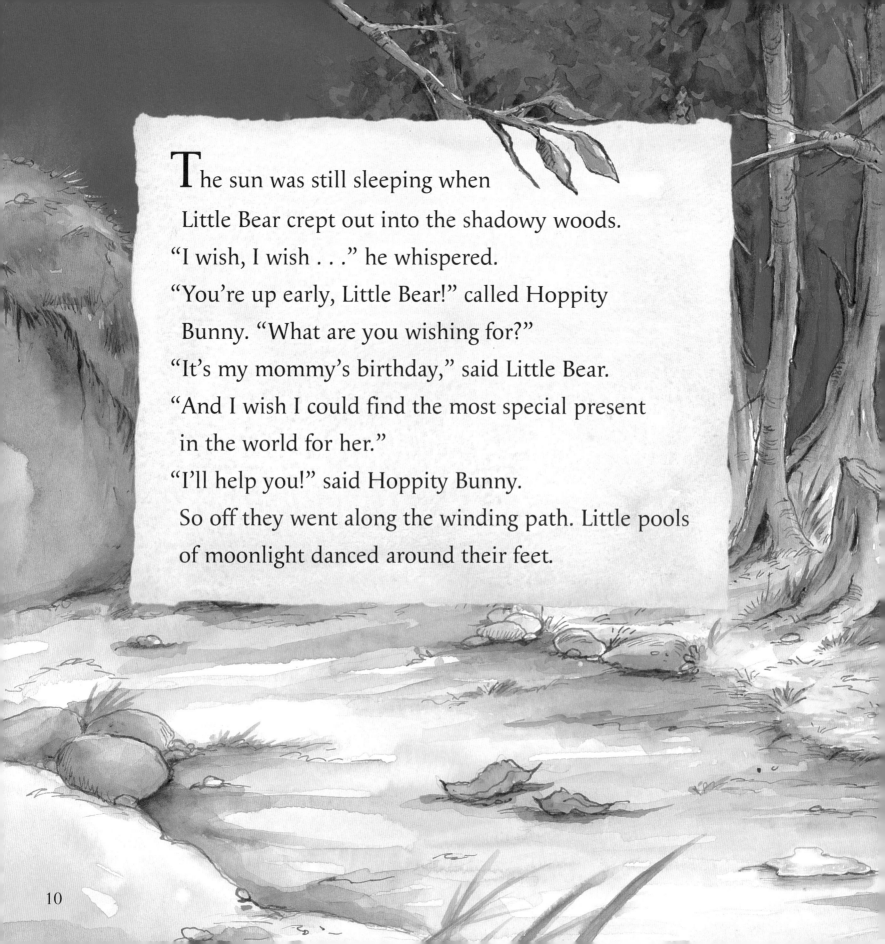

The sun was still sleeping when
Little Bear crept out into the shadowy woods.
"I wish, I wish . . ." he whispered.
"You're up early, Little Bear!" called Hoppity
Bunny. "What are you wishing for?"
"It's my mommy's birthday," said Little Bear.
"And I wish I could find the most special present
in the world for her."
"I'll help you!" said Hoppity Bunny.
So off they went along the winding path. Little pools
of moonlight danced around their feet.

In the middle of the woods was a big rock.

Little Bear sat down for a minute to think.

High above him glittered a star, so big and

bright he could almost touch it.

"I know! I could give my mommy a star,"

he said. "That would be a very special present."

Little Bear gave
a little jump. But he
could not reach the star.

He gave a very big jump.
But still he could not reach
the star. Then Little
Bear had an idea.

"I know!" he said. "If we climb to the very top of the hill, then we will be able to reach the stars!"

From the top of the hill the stars looked even brighter—and much closer, too. Little Bear stretched up onto his tiptoes. But the stars were still too far away. Then Little Bear had an even better idea.

"I know what we can do!" he said. "We can build
a big, big tower to the stars!"
"I'll help you!" said
Hoppity Bunny.

Together they piled the biggest stones they could find,
one on top of the other. Then they stepped back and looked.
A stone stairway stretched to the stars. "Now I can reach
a star for my mommy," said Little Bear happily.
He climbed right to the top and stretched out a paw.
But still he could not reach the stars.

"I have an idea!" called Hoppity Bunny. "If I climb

onto your shoulders, then I can knock a star

out of the sky with my long ears!"

Hoppity Bunny scrambled up to Little Bear's

shoulders. He stretched his long ears

up to the sky. He waved his ears furiously.

"Be careful, Hoppity!" called Little Bear.

"You're making me wobble!"

Suddenly Little Bear felt
someone tapping on his foot.
   "Can I help you?" croaked a voice.
   "Yes, I think you can, Green Frog,"
   said Little Bear. "Aren't you
   a good jumper?"
   Green Frog puffed out his chest.
   "Just watch me!" he said.
High into the air he leaped,
and landed right between
   Hoppity Bunny's long ears.

   "Can you reach the brightest star from there?"
   asked Little Bear.
   "No problem!" shouted Green Frog.
   He took a deep breath. "Look out, stars!"
   he shouted. "Here I come!"

Green Frog gave a great push with his strong
back legs. Up, up, up he sailed. Hoppity Bunny's
long ears twirled around and around.
"Help!" he shouted. "Somebody save me!"
Backward and forward swayed Hoppity, and
backward and forward swayed Little Bear. With a
mighty crash the stone tower toppled to the ground,
and down tumbled Hoppity Bunny and Little Bear.

"I can't breathe!" gasped Little Bear.
"You're sitting right on my nose!"

Then Green Frog sailed down from the
sky and landed on Hoppity Bunny's head.
"I'm sorry Little Bear," he said. "I jumped
right over the moon, but I still
could not reach the stars."

Little Bear sat up carefully.

His nose was scratched and his head hurt.

"My special wish will never come true,"

he said. "I'll never find a star for my mommy!"

"Don't be sad, Little Bear," said Hoppity Bunny.

And he gave Little Bear a big hug.

A tear ran down Little Bear's nose and

splashed into a tiny puddle at his feet.

As Little Bear rubbed his eyes, he saw
something dancing and sparkling in
the tiny puddle. It must be his star!
Little Bear jumped up with excitement.
"I know what I can do to get a star!" he cried.

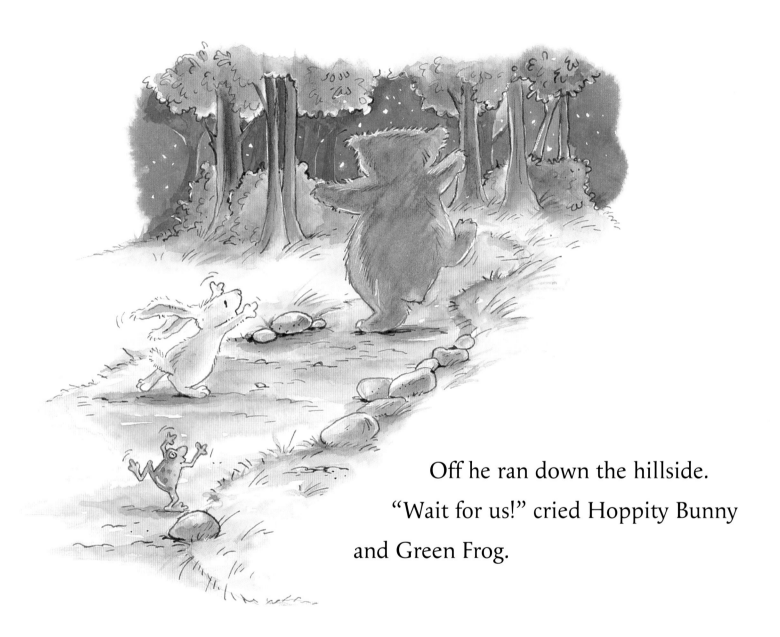

Off he ran down the hillside.
"Wait for us!" cried Hoppity Bunny
and Green Frog.

They all ran through the woods and across the dewy
meadows until they reached the stream, silvery in
the moonlight. For a long time they searched along
the sandy shore until Little Bear found just what
he was looking for. Then, very carefully, he
carried his special thing all the way home.

31

"Happy birthday, Mommy!" cried Little Bear.
He placed a pearly shell that shone like a rainbow
into his mother's lap. In the heart of the shell,
a tiny pool of water quivered. And in that pool a
very special star shimmered and shook—the star
that had made a little bear's birthday wish come true.
"Hoppity Bunny and Green Frog helped me find
the shell, but I caught the star all by myself!" said
Little Bear proudly.
Mommy Bear knelt down and gave Little Bear a
big hug. "Thank you all very much," she said.
"This is a very special birthday present."

newton

by

Rory Tyger

CREAK, CREAK, CRE-E-EAK

Newton woke up suddenly.
There was a funny noise somewhere in the
room. "Don't be frightened," he told Woffle.
"There's always an explanation for everything."
He gave each of his toys a special cuddle
so they wouldn't be scared.

CREAK, CREAK, CRE-E-EAK

went the noise again.

Newton got out of bed and turned on the light.
He walked across the room . . .

"See, toys," he said. "There's nothing to be frightened of. It's only the closet door!"

Newton went back to bed again.

FLAP! FLAP! FLAP!

What was that? Was it a ghost?

Once more Newton got out of bed. He wasn't really scared, but he took his bravest toy, Snappy, just in case. He tiptoed, very quietly, toward the noise.

FLAP! FLAP! FLAP!

it went again. "Of course!" said Newton . . .

"Just what I thought."
It was his bedroom curtains,
flapping in the breeze.
"I'll take care of this,"
said Newton.

"You were very brave,
Snappy," he said, as
he closed the window.

SPLISH!
SPLASH!
SPLISH!

Another noise!

Newton looked outside. It wasn't raining.
Besides, the noise wasn't coming from
outside.

Nor was it coming from his bedroom. What was it? "Stay right there, you two," said Newton, "while I look around."

He wasn't the tiniest bit afraid. He was just taking Snappy with him for company.

Newton crept down the corridor. It was
very spooky, especially in the dark corners.

SPLISH! SPLASH! SPLISH!
went the noise.

Very, very quietly, Newton
opened the bathroom door . . .

"Of course, we knew it was the bathroom
faucet, didn't we, Snappy," said Newton.

Newton turned off the faucet, and
tiptoed back down the hallway.
"Shh," he said to Snappy, just
in case *something* in the dark
corners sprang out at them.

Before he got into bed, Newton pulled back the curtains—just to check. It was very, very quiet outside. "No more funny noises," said Newton.

"You can go to sleep now," he told all his toys.

RUMBLE! RUMBLE! RUMBLE!

"Oh no!" cried Newton. "What's that?"

Newton listened very hard. Not a sound. He was just beginning to think he hadn't heard anything at all when

RUMBLE! RUMBLE! RUMBLE!

There it was again!

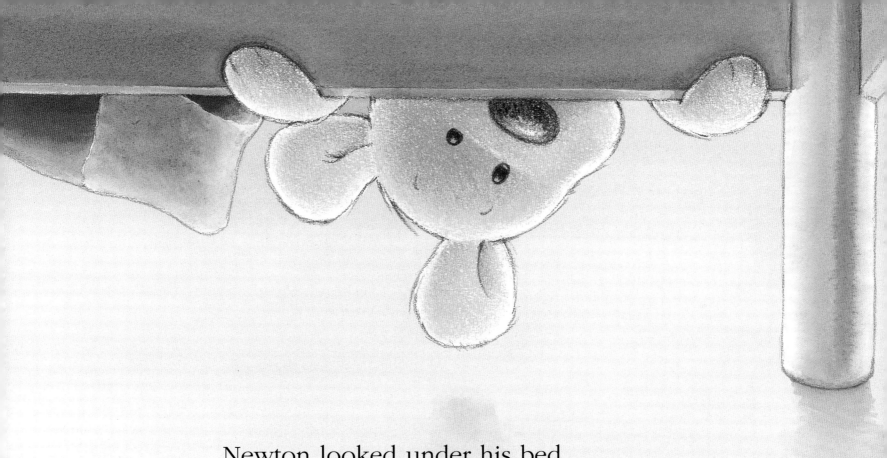

Newton looked under his bed.
Nothing there at all—except for
an old candy he'd forgotten about.
"Don't worry," said Newton. "We'll
soon find out what it is."

RUMBLE!
Newton stood
very still.

RUMBLE!
Newton listened
very hard.

RUMBLE! went the noise.
And suddenly Newton knew
exactly what it was!

Newton padded downstairs, and into the kitchen. He helped himself to a large glass of milk and two thick slices of bread and honey. And now he could hear no

RUMBLE! RUMBLE! RUMBLE!

at all, because . . .

the rumbling had been
his empty tummy!

Newton went upstairs again, and told his toys
about his rumbling tummy.
"There's always an explanation for everything,"
said Newton, as he climbed back into bed.
"Goodnight, everyone . . ."

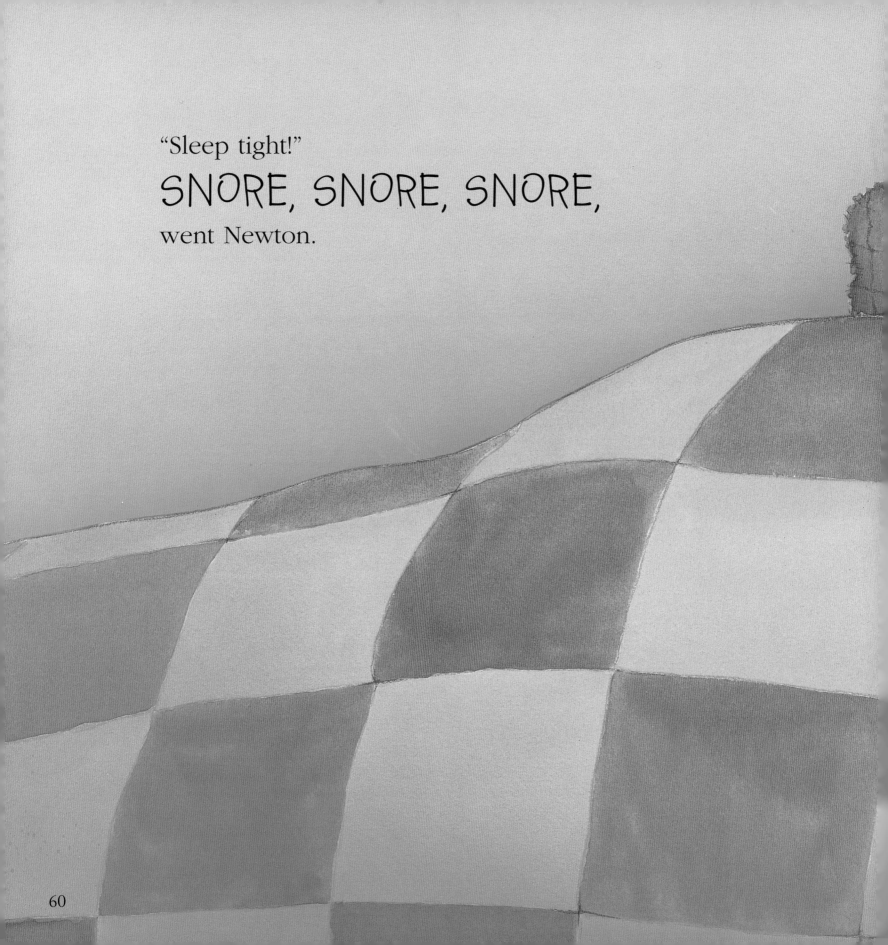

"Sleep tight!"
SNORE, SNORE, SNORE,
went Newton.

60

Have you got my Purr?

by
Judy West and Tim Warnes

"Oh Mommy, Mommy!"

"What's the matter, little Kitten?

Why are you crying?"

"Oh Mommy, Mommy, I've lost my purr."

"You'll find your purr, little Kitten.

Just wait and see."

"Oh Dog, Dog, have you got my purr?"

"Woof, woof," said Dog, licking his bone.

"I haven't got your purr, little Kitten.

This is my *woof*. Why don't you ask Cow?"

"Oh Cow, Cow, have
you got my purr?"
"Moo, moo," said Cow,
flicking flies with
her ears.

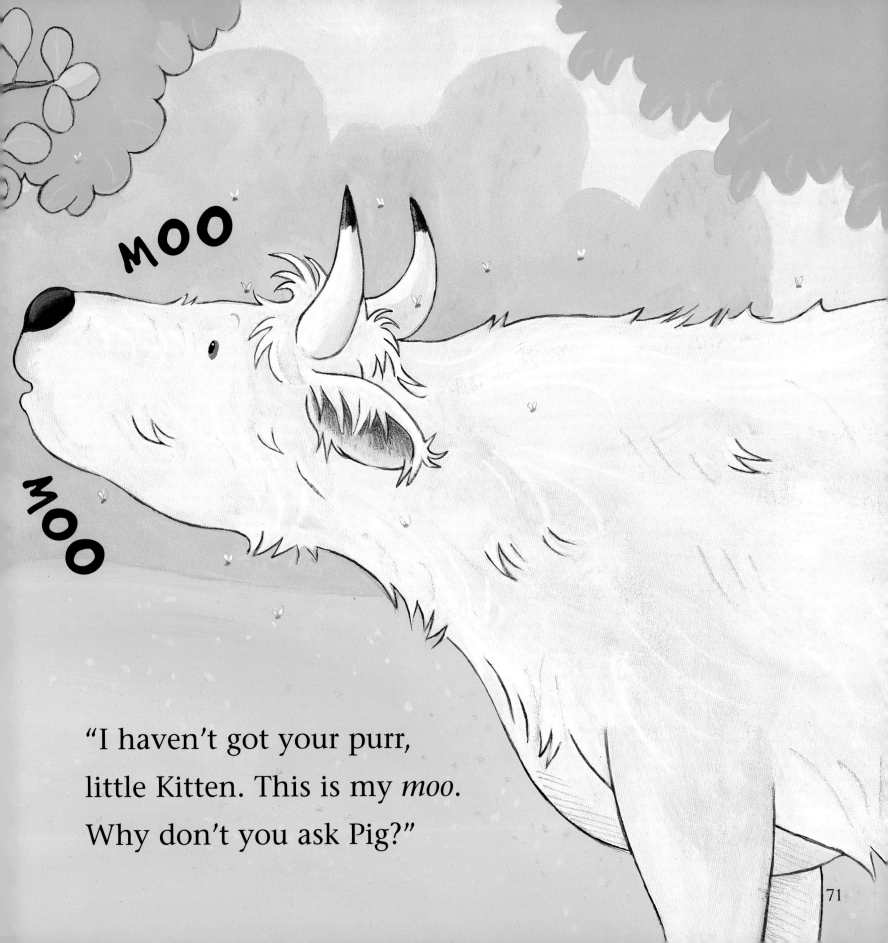

"I haven't got your purr, little Kitten. This is my *moo*. Why don't you ask Pig?"

71

"Oh Pig, Pig, have you got my purr?"
"Oink, oink," said Pig, snuffling
in the straw.

"I haven't got your purr, little Kitten. This is my *oink*. Why don't you ask Duck?"

"Oh Duck, Duck, have you
got my purr?"
"Quack, quack," said Duck,
splashing in the water.

"I haven't got your purr, little Kitten. This is my *quack*. Why don't you ask Mouse?"

"Oh Mouse, Mouse, have you got my purr?"
"Squeak, squeak," said Mouse, nibbling cheese
in the barn. "I haven't got your purr, little Kitten.
This is my *squeak*. Why don't you ask Sheep?"

SQUEAK
SQUEAK

"Oh Sheep, Sheep, have you got my purr?"
"Baa, baa," said Sheep, munching grass in
the field. "I haven't got your purr, little Kitten.
This is my *baa*. Why don't you ask wise old Owl?"

79

"Wise old Owl, have you got my purr?"
"Hoot, hoot," said the wise old Owl, blinking his big round eyes.

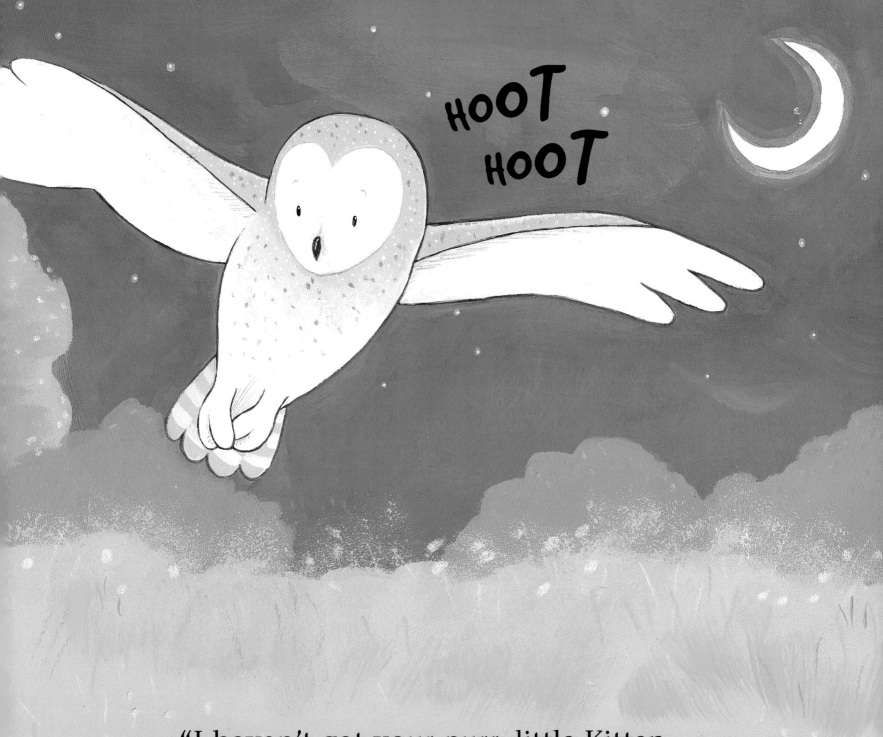

HOOT
HOOT

"I haven't got your purr, little Kitten.
This is my *hoot*. Why don't you go
back and ask your mommy?"

"Oh Mommy, Mommy," wailed little Kitten. "*Nobody's* got my purr. Dog hasn't got it. He's got a woof. Cow hasn't got it. She's got a moo. Pig hasn't got it. She's got an oink. Duck hasn't got it. She's got a quack. Mouse hasn't got it. He's got a squeak. Sheep hasn't got it. She's got a baa. Wise old Owl hasn't got it. He's got a hoot. Oh Mommy, Mommy, I've lost my purr!"

"You haven't lost your purr,
little Kitten. Come here
and I'll explain."

"Nobody's got your purr.
Your purr is inside you
when you're happy!
Listen, little Kitten,
listen . . ."

86

"My *purr!*
Oh, Mommy.
I've found my purr!
It was here
all the time."
So little Kitten
curled up . . .

and purred and purred
and purred.

PURR PURR

GOODNIGHT, LITTLE HARE

Sheridan Cain

illustrated by
Sally Percy

By the pale light of the moon, Mother Hare
sat watching Little Hare. He lay with eyes tightly
shut. For his blanket he had the sky, and the
soft hay formed his bed.

"Goodnight, Little Hare," she whispered.

Mole happened by and almost toppled over Little Hare. "Mother Hare," he said, "you cannot leave your baby there. It isn't safe, for the farmer cuts the hay at dawn."

"But what can I do?" asked Mother Hare. "Where can Little Hare sleep?"

"You should dig a hole, big and deep," said Mole. "That's where your little baby should sleep."

So Mother Hare began to dig.

She scraped and scraped
at the soft, brown earth, until
the hole was big and deep. Then
she carried Little Hare to his new bed.

But Little Hare did not like it. "Mama," he cried. "It's so dark and I'm afraid."

Badger came bumbling along and heard
Little Hare's cry. "Mother Hare," he said,
"you cannot leave your baby there. It isn't safe.
Weasel is hunting through hole and burrow,
and he will soon find Little Hare."

"But what can I do?" asked Mother Hare.
"Where can Little Hare sleep?"
"You should cover him in a bed of
leaves. That will fool Weasel,"
said Badger.

101

So Mother Hare hurried
and scurried.

She formed the leaves
into a soft, round pile.
Then she carried Little
Hare to his new bed.

But Little Hare did not like it.
"Mama," he cried. "I'm so afraid. I don't like
the crinkly, crackly noise my new bed makes."

Blackbird was up early, pecking among the
leaves for grubs when he heard Little Hare's cry.

"Mother Hare," he said, "you cannot leave your
baby there. It isn't safe. Fox's nose is sharp
and he will soon sniff out Little Hare."

"But what can I do?" asked Mother Hare.

"Where can Little Hare sleep?"

"What you need is a nest
up high," said Blackbird.

"Fox will never reach
him there."

So Mother Hare leapt up
onto the branch of a tree,
and placed Little Hare
in an empty bird's nest.

But Little Hare did not like it.
"Mama," he cried, looking down.
"I'm so afraid. It's high up here
and I might fall out."

107

Mother Hare carried Little Hare down
again. She did not know what to do.
"Oh dear," she sobbed. "How can
I find a bed that's safe
for Little Hare?"

109

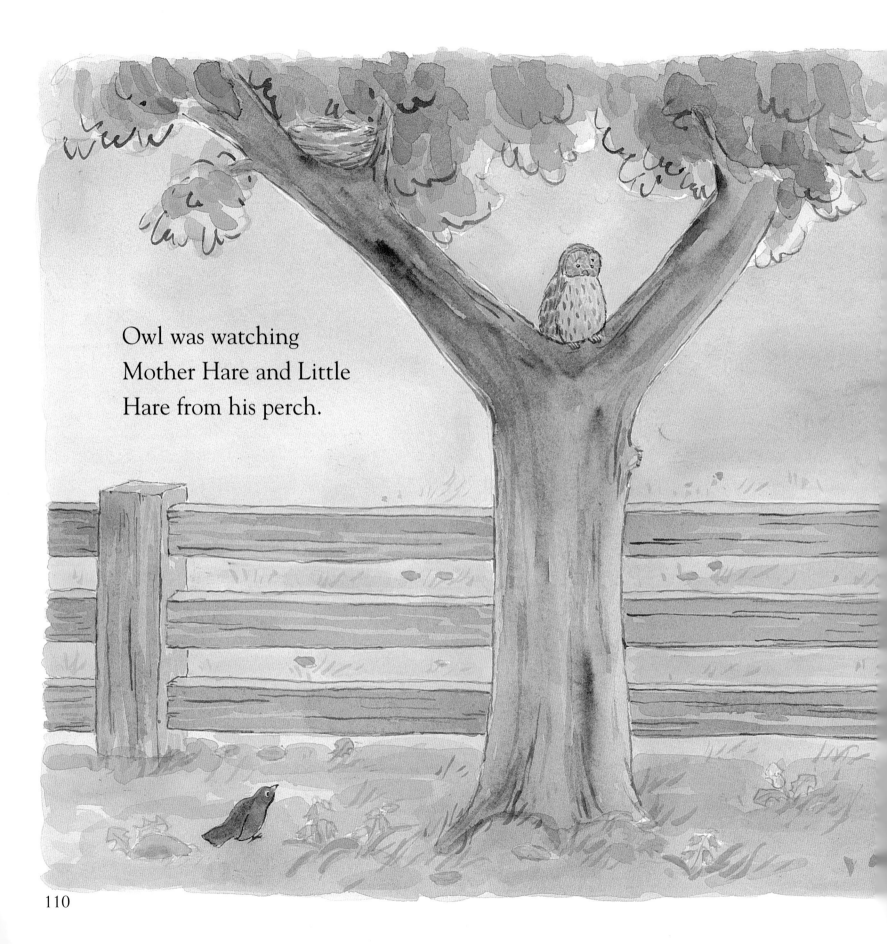

Owl was watching
Mother Hare and Little
Hare from his perch.

110

"Don't be sad," said Owl.
"Don't you remember when *you*
were young, and how *your* mother
kept you safe?"

112

Mother Hare remembered the sky
that was her blanket. She remembered
the soft, golden hay that was her bed.

She remembered how, from
dusk to dawn, her mother
had watched over her.

The sun was just rising.
Mother Hare looked
towards the field that
was her home and her
eyes became bright. The
farmer had come early
and the hay was cut.
It was quite safe
there now.

Mother Hare carried
Little Hare back to his
old bed and laid him
gently down.

"Mama," said Little Hare.
"I'm not afraid now. This
is my own bed and I like it."

Goodnight, Little Hare!

117